TRAPPED!

You're following a narrow trail that winds through a forest. Rounding a bend, you see a giant spider several feet high. You pick up a heavy stick from the forest floor. Little use! Ahead is a whole army of giant spiders, and there are more behind you.

You stumble into the forest, hoping you'll reach a straight trail. You hear voices ahead. But your heart sinks: they're crogocides! If they see you, they'll enslave you—but they may be your only hope.

WILL YOU ESCAPE FROM
TENOPIA ISLAND?

When—and if—you do, more challenges await you on the planet Tenopia.

You can continue your escape adventures in these books, coming soon:

#2: TRAPPED IN THE SEA KINGDOM
#3: TERROR ON KABRAN
#4: STAR SYSTEM TENOPIA

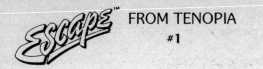

Escape™ FROM TENOPIA
#1

TENOPIA ISLAND

by Edward Packard

Illustrated by David Perry

BANTAM BOOKS
TORONTO · NEW YORK · LONDON · SYDNEY · AUCKLAND

RL 5, IL age 10 and up

TENOPIA ISLAND
A Bantam Book / June 1986
*Escape is a trademark of
Metabooks, Inc.*

Cover art by Catherine Huerta

ISBN 0-553-25472-3

Published simultaneously in the United States and Canada

Bantam Books are published by Bantam Books, Inc. Its trademark, consisting of the words "Bantam Books" and the por-
trayal of a rooster, is Registered in U.S. Patent and Trademark
Office and in other countries. Marca Registrada. Bantam
Books, Inc., 666 Fifth Avenue, New York, New York 10103.

PRINTED IN THE UNITED STATES OF AMERICA

O   0 9 8 7 6 5 4 3 2 1

TENOPIA ISLAND

NOTICE!!!

You are about to find yourself trapped on a strange and dangerous island on one of the most forbidding planets in the galaxy: Tenopia. It's important that you follow the directions in this book if you hope to escape!

During your travels on Tenopia Island, you'll have a small computer that can project a map of the region you're in at any moment. To use this, flip to the map page indicated near the bottom of the page you're reading. (When you turn to a map page, be sure to keep a finger on the page you're reading so you won't lose your place.)

Whether or not you escape from Tenopia Island will depend on how skillful you are, how persistent you are, and how lucky you are. Will you succeed—or will you be trapped forever? It's entirely up to you!

While you are traveling on a diplomatic mission from Earth to the Mylaean Cluster, your spaceship is hit by a meteor. With seconds to spare, you jettison in an escape pod, the only survivor. The pod's built-in computer indicates there is only enough fuel to reach Tenopia, the fifth planet of Star System Tenopia. The computer's memory bank supplies you with the following information:

> TENOPIA: 4/5 Earth size; rotation 26 hours; sun rises in the east, sets in west; revolution 587 days; air quality excellent; food and water abundant; surface 80% ocean with one large island (Tenopia Island) and a single continent (Kabran); ocean is subject to violent storms; galactic language widely spoken; technology generally medieval; travel dangerous and not advised.

Bracing yourself for entry into Tenopia's atmosphere, you examine your only survival equipment— a pocket-sized computer that is programmed to project a map of your region at all times on a small video screen.

Suddenly, on the pod's computer, you read:

> Entry Phase: landing targeted near Krelia, west coast of Tenopia Island.

A moment later the words "Tenopia Island" appear, and this aerial view is displayed:

Go on to the next page.

TENOPIA
ISLAND

Go on to the next page.

4

Your tiny craft sets down with a sharp jolt. You lie dazed for a few minutes before you can pull yourself together. By the time you crawl through the hatch, your pod is already surrounded by giant half-human creatures with huge forked hands. They blindfold you and lead you along a winding bumpy surface, then down a long ladder that leads deep underground. At last they remove your blindfold. You are in a huge dimly lit cavern that reeks of sulfurous fumes.

The creatures search you. You hold your breath when they find your computer. But they toss it aside as a useless ornament, and you're able to retrieve it a few moments later.

You quickly learn that your captors are crogocides and that you have been condemned to slavery in their krelium mine. Closely watched by crogocide guards wielding long spiked sticks, you are forced to chip and shovel krelium ore for seven hours before you're allowed to rest for the night.

Most of the slaves speak the galactic language, and during the days that follow you make friends with Prespar, an old hominid from a nearby planet. He looks almost as human as yourself.

When you ask whether there is any hope of escape from the mine, Prespar merely shakes his head. But that night, while there are no crogocides nearby, he comes to you and whispers, "There is a secret tunnel that leads to the surface. Tomorrow I will show you the slab that hides the entrance."

"How do I get to the nearest galactic patrol station?" you whisper back.

Turn to page 10.

A few minutes later, three crogocides seize you. Blindfolded, hands tied behind your back, you're transported by cart and by boat and again by cart to the krelium mine. There you are set to the same grueling work—chipping and shoveling, chipping and shoveling.

This time you're watched more closely than ever by the crogocide guards. Several days pass before you have a chance to pull back the slab covering the secret tunnel.

Your heart is in your mouth because you're afraid you'll find the passageway sealed off. But it's still open! Soon you're standing once again on the surface of Tenopia! You're only at the beginning of your journey, but at least you know a lot more than before.

TO CHECK MAP, SEE PAGE 17.

If you head northeast, turn to page 20.

If you head south, turn to page 16.

Once again you have reached the encampment of the red-winged bird people.

Kumba steps forward and greets you. "We had hoped you would be well on your way to Zindor by now."

"It doesn't look as if I'm making very good progress," you say.

Kumba rests a wing on your shoulder. "I think you'll have better luck if you head south to the Rapoor River. The crogocides are gone, and the southern route is clear now. I can show you the way to a trail that leads through the forest."

"Thanks, I'll try it," you quickly reply.

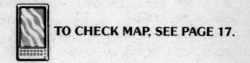 **TO CHECK MAP, SEE PAGE 17.**

Turn to page 44.

As you continue on your way, you find good fruit and nuts, and spongy leaves that taste like bananas. You rest on the mossy banks of a stream and marvel at the lush plants. A village lies ahead. As you approach it, you are alarmed by screams and sounds of fighting.

If you have been to Anarchia before, turn to page 23. If not, read on. . . .

Keeping carefully out of sight, you look for a road leading out of town. Rocks rain down from the roof of a house. You duck into an alley, almost colliding with a bird child who looks so much like a big parrot that you want to laugh.

Apparently the child thinks *you're* funny, because he laughs. "My name is Nem," he says. "You are in Anarchia—the worst place on Tenopia Island. If you don't leave in a hurry, you won't survive."

"Well, how do I leave?"

Turn to page 12.

"First you must escape from this island. You'll have a long and difficult journey," says Prespar, "much too long for these old bones. The only station is on Kabran, which lies on the other side of an ocean subject to storms so violent they sink every ship that tries to cross it."

"Then how can I get there?"

"Only by balloon. And the only balloon on Tenopia Island is possessed by my friend Kin Rugg, who lives far to the east in a tiny village beyond Lake Shonra. It's called Zindor, but you'll not find it on any map; the crogocides have never dared to go near there."

"Will Kin Rugg take me to Kabran?"

Prespar nods. "I once saved his life, and he promised to do any favor I asked. I'll give you a letter to bring to him. He will understand that I am too old to go."

"Thank you a thousand times, Prespar. Is there anything else I should know?"

Prespar looks anxiously around. "You will encounter many creatures on this island, some friendly, some dangerous. You can trust the bird people—they do not fly, but their wings are like feathered hands, as nimble as yours and mine. Look for the prince of Agron. He will help you. Most of all, beware of the crogocides! They enslave every hominid that can hold a shovel and swing a pick."

Go on to the next page.

"How can I travel about?"

"The crogocides ride zekees, shaggy animals with curved horns, but you will probably have to walk, unless you can get aboard a coastal ship at one of the seaports." Again Prespar looks nervously around. "Oh, one thing more—*never, never set foot on Cape Mori.*"

"Where's that?"

Suddenly Prespar turns away. Two guards are approaching. You quickly pretend to be asleep, resolving that before another day passes you will be free.

Turn to page 14.

12

Beckoning you to follow, Nem leads you through twisting alleys to the edge of town. The road ahead branches into two trails.

"The trail to the east is very dangerous," he tells you. "It leads through the Land of the Diving Birds. It would be safer to take the road leading south."

 TO CHECK MAP, SEE PAGE 21.

If you go south to avoid the diving birds, turn to page 31.

If you decide to take your chances with the diving birds, turn to page 28.

14

Early the next morning, at a moment when no guards are looking, Prespar pulls back the slab that hides the entrance to the secret tunnel. You quickly shake his hand and slip through the narrow opening. After a long and difficult climb in total darkness, you reach the surface and gratefully breathe the fresh clean air. A dirt road stretches out like a ribbon in both directions. A warm breeze is blowing. Birds are singing. You feel encouraged.

The landscape is covered with lush plants bearing tiny flowers that are tinted by the glow from the huge orange sun. Though four or five times as big in the sky as the Earth's sun, you can look right at it without hurting your eyes!

Holding your computer, you display a map of the region. You can see that the road leads to the northeast through open meadows, to the south through dense forest. You're inclined to go northeast because your goal, Zindor, lies to the east. But it might be wise to go south; the forest would give you better protection from any pursuing guards.

 TO CHECK MAP, SEE PAGE 17.

If you head northeast, turn to page 20.

If you head south, turn to page 16.

This time, you look for the road leading out of Kacita to the south. But first, out of curiosity, you seek out the bird man in the mirrored robe. Though still silent, he seems glad to see you and writes this on his slate:

**ZINDOR IS IN
THE LAVA FIELDS**

Soon you're on the road once again.

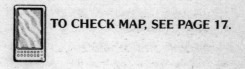 **TO CHECK MAP, SEE PAGE 17.**

Turn to page 86.

As you walk along the road, the orange sunlight streaming through yellow-leafed trees produces a misty light like nothing you've ever seen. After several hours of travel, you hear weird, rhythmic music ahead—a chorus of voices running up and down the scale, changing from dissonance to harmony.

If you have visited the red-winged bird people before, turn to page 8. If not, read on. . . .

You are drawn to the sound, but before you can reach its source, two bird people with dark red wings spring from behind a tree. The music stops, and in a moment a dozen more bird people gather around you. They seem friendly, and you waste no time in telling them of your quest for Zindor.

Their leader, Kumba, listens attentively. "You wish to go to Zindor? I can only tell you this. If you ever reach the village of Issus on the shore of Lake Shonra, you will see a signpost with three signs. Follow the sign that is most different from the other two."

Turn to page 19.

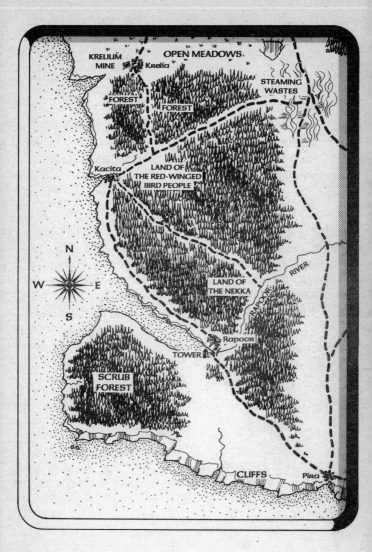

As you thank Kumba for this information, a lookout runs toward you. "The crogocides are coming from the south!"

"They may be looking for you," Kumba says. "You must leave at once. I know you want to go east, but that way leads to the steaming wastes. If you go south, you'll run straight into the crogocides. I think it's better to go west, toward Kacita."

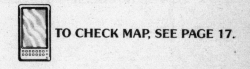 **TO CHECK MAP, SEE PAGE 17.**

*If you take a chance on going east,
turn to page 31.*

*If you play it safe and head west, toward Kacita,
turn to page 24.*

You hurry along the road leading northeast. Every once in a while you look back to see if the crogocides are following, but the road is clear. After some time the road forks to the right. Up ahead is a bridge that crosses the river Kree. A new map appears on your screen; you check it for clues as to which way to go.

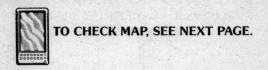 **TO CHECK MAP, SEE NEXT PAGE.**

If you take the road to the right, to Anarchia, turn to page 9.

If you continue straight ahead across the river to Blu, turn to page 26.

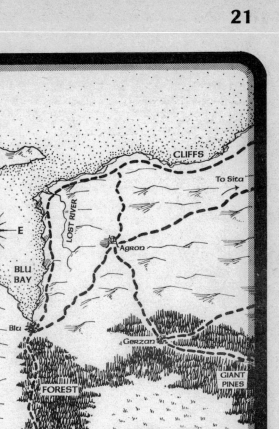
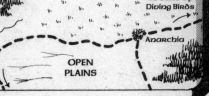

You've arrived once again at Anarchia. You feel lucky to have gotten out alive before, and you don't intend to hang around.

Looking at your map, you notice that Agron is due north. At the same time you remember that Prespar said that the prince of Agron could help you. There's no road leading north, but you can use the orange sun as your compass, and the terrain is fairly flat and mostly unwooded. You have a good meal of berries and breadfruit gathered from plants along the way and, with the midday sun at your back, set out across the countryside.

 TO CHECK MAP, SEE PAGE 21.

Turn to page 39.

The moment you see the attractive stone houses of Kacita, and the markets filled with a great variety of fruits and vegetables, your spirits rise.

If you have already been to Kacita, turn to page 15. If not, read on. . . .

The people seem friendly, but they will not speak. You wonder if they are bound by a vow of silence. You can tell by signs over doorways that they know how to read and write, but their print seems almost impossible to read.

You wander down narrow twisting alleys trying to find your way to the docks. A bird man wearing a gray hooded robe embroidered with little mirrors catches your eye. Hoping he might be willing to talk, you ask if he knows how you can get to Zindor.

He says nothing but takes out a slate and writes on it.

You can't quite read the words he's written, but the letters look strangely familiar.

ⱯHTꟼMAⱵƎꓘAWAHꓳ ꓷИIꟻ

Looking at your map, you decide to avoid the road to the steaming wastes.

There are two other roads leading out of town, one leading south and one leading southeast.

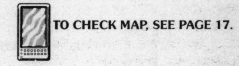 **TO CHECK MAP, SEE PAGE 17.**

If you follow the road southeast, turn to page 44.

If you follow the road south, turn to page 86.

26

You cross the river Kree and eventually reach the village of Blu. The bird people who live here tell you that Blu Harbor is too shallow for big boats, but that you might be able to get a boat to the east end of the island by traveling farther up the coast.

"What about Agron, to the northeast of here?" you ask, after consulting your map.

"Agron," one of them says, "is the castle of the hominid prince, whose fortress protects him from the crogocides. If he decides you were sent by the crogocides, he will throw you in the dungeon!"

 TO CHECK MAP, SEE PAGE 21.

*If you continue north along the coast,
turn to page 37.*

If you head toward Agron, turn to page 33.

The prince listens with interest as you recount the events that brought you to Tenopia and of your search for Zindor. "Ah, Zindor," he sighs. "Besides this fortress, Zindor is the only place on the island that is safe from the crogocides. It lies nestled in the lava fields on the eastern slopes of the great Keona Volcano. Although the volcano has been dormant for many years, it rumbles and smokes from time to time, and the crogocides are afraid to go near it."

"How would one reach the volcano?" you ask.

"Well," says the prince, scratching his furry chin, "the volcano lies far to the southeast of here, beyond Gerzan. But if you go southeast, you risk being captured by crogocides. It would be safer to go northeast to Sita, and hope to find your way from there."

 TO CHECK MAP, SEE PAGE 21.

If you go northeast to Sita, turn to page 68.

If you risk going southeast to Gerzan, turn to page 38.

You travel through rolling meadows spotted with gigantic pine trees, their needles as big as baseball bats. You've trekked several miles when you hear a sound like a foghorn, rising in pitch to a piercing shriek. Looking up at the sky, you see a great blue bird, larger than any you have seen on Earth. It's diving right at you, its mighty talons like fishhooks about to dig into your shoulders and neck!

You jump wildly out of its path, and the great bird lands with a thump that shakes the ground. You run a few steps, wondering if you can make it to the woods. The bird laboriously hops in the direction of the wind, flapping mightily, and is barely able to get airborne. Slowly it gains altitude, then circles above you. You judge that you can duck out of the way if it dives again. But more of the huge birds are flying your way. Should you go southeast and hope you can dodge them, or cut to the northeast through the dense woods? A new map appears on your screen. You consult it in hopes of finding clues.

 **TO CHECK MAP, SEE NEXT PAGE.**

If you go northeast, turn to page 92.

If you go southeast, turn to page 50.

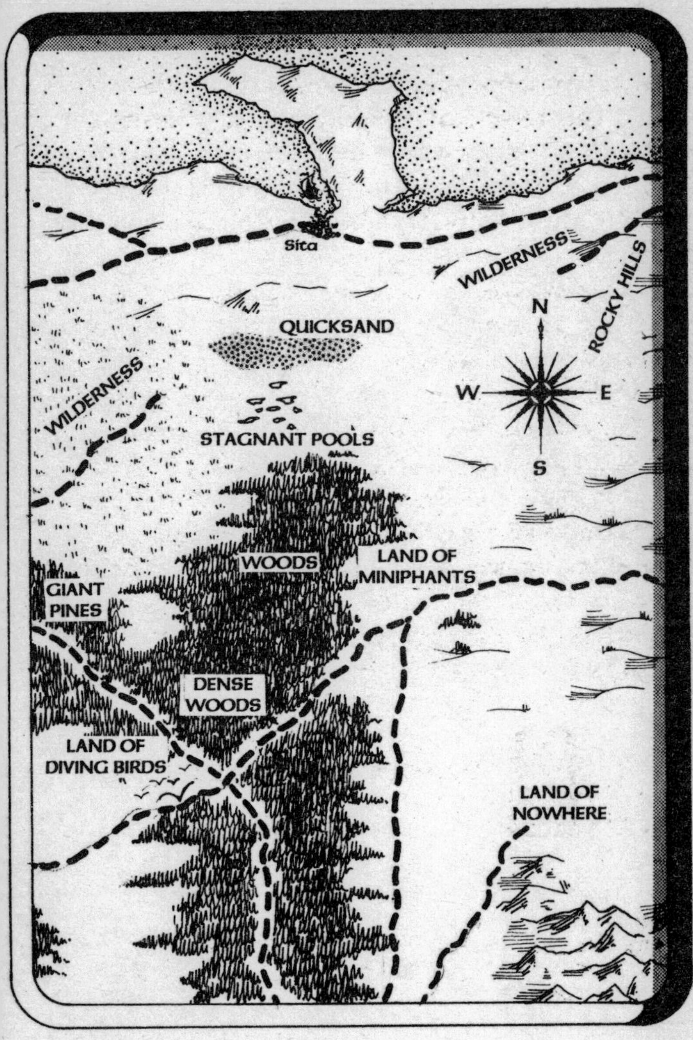
Sita
WILDERNESS
ROCKY HILLS
N
QUICKSAND
WILDERNESS
W
E
STAGNANT POOLS
S
WOODS
LAND OF
MINIPHANTS
GIANT
PINES
DENSE
WOODS
LAND OF
DIVING BIRDS
LAND OF
NOWHERE

After hiking most of the day, you come over a rise. Ahead, you see a desert pocketed with pools of bubbling water. Steam and mists rise above it like ghostly corkscrews. The air stinks of sulfur. Soon you're gasping for breath.

You wend your way through the steaming wastes, but the fumes and heat are too much for you. Reluctantly, you turn back. You must go around this wasteland. either to the north or to the south.

 TO CHECK MAP, SEE PAGE 17.

If you head north, turn to page 9.

If you head south, turn to page 44.

After a long hike over a narrow winding road, you spot Agron Castle, perched on a hill that rises from the plains like an upside-down bowl.

If you have been to Agron before, turn to page 77. If not, read on. . . .

Surrounded by a high stone wall, the great castle looks invulnerable to any force of arms that could be mustered on Tenopia Island. A small furry-bodied guard dressed in a gray uniform and armed with a sharp spear stops you at the gate.

"Please, I am a stranger to this island. I need help," you say.

After conferring with some other guards, he leads you into the castle itself, through a broad courtyard and up winding stone stairs to the main gallery. There you sit and wait until you are so tired you nearly fall asleep. Suddenly the prince of Agron, followed by guards and courtiers, strides into the room. With his luxuriant fur and broad square body, he seems imposing but not threatening.

Turn to page 27.

Once again you find yourself in the crystal mine, chipping the walls of the cave, shoveling bits of crystal into a cart that another slave wheels away.

As soon as you have the chance, you look around. Nearby you spot a cart loaded with tiny bits of crystal. Taking a chance the guards won't see you, you burrow in under the crystal chips until you are completely out of sight. Soon the cart begins to move. When it does, the crystal chips dig in from beneath you. Every inch of your skin pricks with pain, but you lie still and keep from crying out. Finally the motion stops. With great care you poke your head above the crystal. You've reached the surface! Your cart is lined up next to others, awaiting transport by river barge. There are no guards about. This is your chance. You quickly check your map.

 TO CHECK MAP, SEE PAGE 53.

If you take the road to the west, turn to page 92.

If you head south, turn to page 52.

If you head north, turn to page 82.

36

You are quickly taken into custody and soon learn that your captors are in service to the prince of Agron.

"Any enemy of the crogocides is a friend of ours," they say.

You gratefully accept their offer to provide boat transportation to the prince's castle, near the extreme northwest part of the island.

On your arrival a few days later, the prince welcomes you in a most kindly manner. After you're well fed and well rested, he sends you on your way with these words: "I have learned that to reach Zindor, you must find Chawakelamptha and then pass through Chiga, and then go south from there. Can you remember all that?"

"I think so," you reply. With renewed hope you set out on your way east.

 TO CHECK MAP, SEE PAGE 21.

Turn to page 68.

After several hours of travel, you cross a dried-up riverbed. A short time later the road curves east, paralleling the cliffs along the coast. From time to time you look down and see huge waves battering the rocks hundreds of feet below.

You're glad to be heading east, but soon a cold gray fog rolls in from the sea. Shivering, you hurry on. A little way farther, you reach a fork in the road. Consulting your map, you decide that the right fork leads to Agron and the left fork continues east along the coast. You would definitely continue east, but the coast road is so cold and foggy you're afraid you'll freeze to death before you reach shelter.

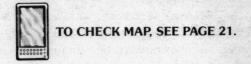 **TO CHECK MAP, SEE PAGE 21.**

If you head toward Agron, turn to page 33.

If you continue east along the coast, turn to page 68.

38

In time, you find yourself approaching the village of Gerzan.

If you have been to Gerzan before, turn to page 45. If not, read on. . . .

Outside the village gates you encounter some bird people loading fruit and vegetables into a cart. One of them, named Teng, warns you that the town is full of crogocides. "You may stay with me in our hut for one night," he says. "Before sunrise tomorrow you must be on your way."

"What road shall I take?" you ask. "I must journey east to Zindor."

"Two roads lead east," says Teng. "The northern one leads through quicksand and then into a vast wilderness, the southern one through the Land of the Diving Birds. In either case you may not survive."

 TO CHECK MAP, SEE PAGE 21.

If you decide to follow the northern route east, turn to page 49.

If you decide to follow the southern route, turn to page 28.

If you decide to go back to Agron, turn to page 77.

Hiking across the rolling meadows, you marvel at the tall golden grass tufted with seed pods that glow like embers in the soft orange sunlight. The seeds themselves taste like bits of honey—a few dozen of them make a decent meal. You're thankful that food is so abundant on Tenopia Island.

From the top of a ridge, you see a lone zekee peacefully nibbling grass. Cautiously you approach and then, with a flash of daring, swing onto its back. Startled, the animal breaks into a gallop. You clutch its shaggy mane and hang on.

There's no chance of steering the animal; you'll just have to go where it goes. You close your eyes and pray you'll survive. The zekee canters over the countryside for almost an hour before it rears up and sends you tumbling into the grass. Dazed, you look around and start walking.

Turn to page 33.

You safely cross the rickety bridge, after which the ground begins to slope steeply upward. But the labor of climbing is more than offset by the joy of breathing the fresh, clean air. Then, from a hilltop peak, you look down.

If you have been to Leata before, turn to page 122. If not, read on. . . .

You see a great basin—a caldera, remnant of the explosion of a volcano. In its center lies a village of humble sod houses dominated by a tower made of thousands of stones. The roof of the tower supports a huge statue of a dragon. According to your map, this village is Leata.

 TO CHECK MAP, SEE NEXT PAGE.

Turn to page 43.

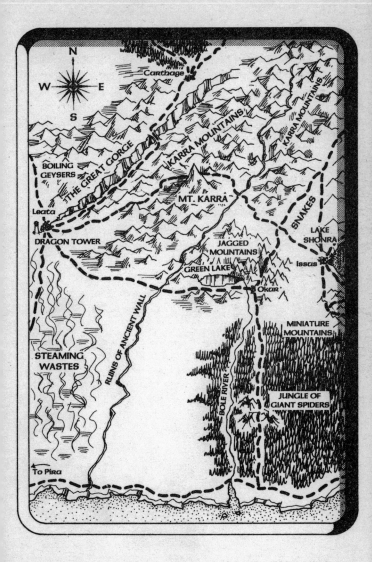

The moment you enter Leata, dozens of bird people hurry toward you, flapping their wings as bird people do to keep their balance while walking.

"Does anyone know the way to Zindor?" you ask.

Your eager new friends all start talking at once:

"If you could take a boat, you would sail to Riva."

"If you could fly, you would fly over Lake Shonra."

"If you could eat fire and smoke, you would cross the Keona Volcano."

Smiling politely, you consult your map for a more helpful clue.

 TO CHECK MAP, SEE PAGE 41.

*If you take the road to Okur,
turn to page 57.*

*If you take the road around Mount Karra,
turn to page 55.*

After traveling through the forest, you reach a settlement of bird people who herd the nekka—shaggy animals from whose soft gray hair the bird people make crude garments and blankets.

You soon make friends with a bird child named Alom, and you ask him if he knows the way to Zindor.

"You would have to cross the Rapoor River," Alom replies. "But the bridge is guarded by crogocides, and you can't swim across."

"I can swim," you say.

Alom shakes his head. "The river is full of zazor fish, and they will eat anything!" He holds his wings outstretched, indicating that a zazor fish is several feet long.

TO CHECK MAP, SEE PAGE 17.

If you try to swim across the Rapoor River,
turn to page 60.

If you head west toward Kacita,
turn to page 24.

To avoid being seen by the crogocides, you sneak into Gerzan at dusk and find the house of your friend Teng.

"You shouldn't have come back," he says. "The crogocides search our houses at all hours of the night. But I do have good news for you. Since you were last here, I have talked to my grandfather. He has been to the far end of the island."

Teng shows you into a house where a bird man lies propped up on cushions in a corner of the room. He is so old his pale yellow skin is stretched tightly over his face.

"Teng says you are searching for Zindor," he murmurs. "I do not know precisely where it is, but I have heard that it is south of Chiga."

Though disappointed at not learning more, you thank Teng and his grandfather and set out on your way. Two trails lead east: one to the northeast, the other to the southeast through the Giant Pines.

 TO CHECK MAP, SEE PAGE 21.

If you follow the northeastern trail, turn to page 49.

If you follow the southeastern trail, turn to page 28.

46

After journeying most of the day, you come upon a stone wall over ten feet tall that extends as far as you can see in both directions.

If you have reached the stone wall before, turn to page 128. If not, read on. . . .

The wall is supported by buttresses spaced a hundred feet or so apart. By getting a grip on the irregular surfaces in the rock, you are able to climb to the top, only to find that your view is blocked by a dense pine forest. If you drop to the ground on the other side, you won't be able to get back.

You wonder: Is this some kind of penal colony or animal reserve? Or could it be a secret route to Zindor? You look at your map and search your memory, thinking of all the things you've learned on your travels on Tenopia Island, before deciding what to do next.

 TO CHECK MAP, SEE NEXT PAGE.

If you jump down on the far side of the wall,
turn to page 111.

If you climb back down the buttress,
turn to page 7.

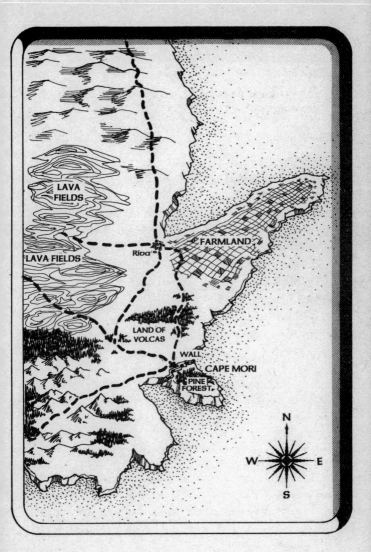

Soon after setting out, you enter the most depressing wilderness you can imagine. There is hardly any vegetation—the land is almost a desert—and yet there are broad stretches of soggy sand and pools of stagnant water. Suddenly you find no support under your feet. In a few seconds you're up to your knees in quicksand. Trying to wade out, you sink deeper still.

You flop over on your back. With your weight now spread over your whole body, you float on the watery sand, and you're able to paddle and roll your way back onto firm ground.

Maybe you should turn back. You shudder at the prospect of being trapped in this wasteland, exhausted and with no chance of finding food. Yet if you turn back, you may wander around the island forever.

You try to move forward, but once again your way is blocked by quicksand.

 **TO CHECK MAP, SEE PAGE 29.**

If you work your way north around the quicksand, turn to page 82.

If you go south, turn to page 92.

Much to your surprise, you have no further trouble along the way. You arrive safely at Carthage, a beautiful town with buildings made of marble slabs arranged in cubes and rectangles. Looking south, you can see the smoky blue outline of the Karra Mountains.

If you have been to Carthage before, go on to the next page. If not, read on. . . .

A family of bird people takes you in with them. They show you the vast quarries from which the marble was removed. You learn that most of the marble was taken out thousands of years ago and lies in cities long since buried by earthquakes.

Your new friends warn you that the way south is blocked by an impassable gorge; the only bridge recently collapsed in a storm. The trail to the northwest is too dangerous, but there are other trails, they say: one to the northeast that leads to the Land of Nowhere, and one to the north that leads to the Land of the Miniphants.

 TO CHECK MAP, SEE PAGE 41.

If you go north to the Land of the Miniphants, turn to page 92.

If you go northeast to the Land of Nowhere, turn to page 61.

In Carthage you find the family that was so kind to you. They tell you that the bridge across the great gorge, leading south, has now been restored, and you decide to follow that route.

 TO CHECK MAP, SEE PAGE 41.

Turn to page 40.

Through woods and meadows you walk, on and on. After a while the land begins rising steeply. Up, up, up you climb, to the summit of Mount Calm. The great orange sun breaks through the fast-moving clouds, giving you a view like none other you've seen on Tenopia Island.

To the west, Mount Friz, far too tall and steep to climb, towers above you. To the south you can see much of Lake Shonra. Far to the southeast is a magnificent snow-capped cone—the Keona Volcano. A curling plume of smoke rises from its summit. To the north is hilly, semiarid country as far as you can see.

You think back over what you've learned so far in your travels, trying to decide which way to go. The land is very rugged; there are only two possible routes.

 **TO CHECK MAP, SEE NEXT PAGE.**

If you head north, turn to page 75.

If you head southwest along the mountain trail, turn to page 65.

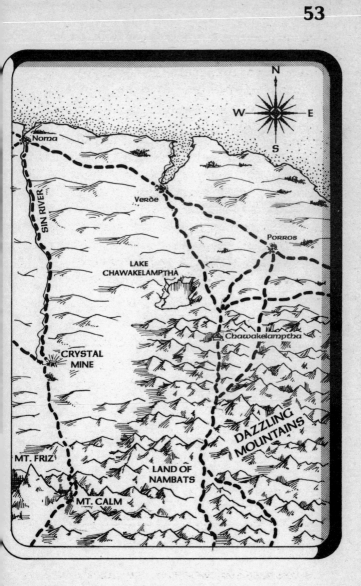

By noon, you reach a high mountain ridge. After descending the steep slope on the far side, you arrive at Issus, a tiny village at the westernmost tip of Lake Shonra. The bird people here offer you fried fish for lunch, but they will not answer your questions about Zindor. You wonder whether they are afraid you might be a crogocide spy.

Then one of the villagers beckons to you. He points to a signpost with three signs, each with an arrow. One arrow points straight ahead, one points to the left, and one points to the right. The three signs look like this:

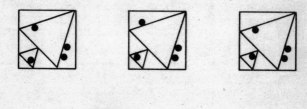

 TO CHECK MAP, SEE PAGE 41.

If you follow the first sign, turn to page 88.

If you follow the second sign, turn to page 62.

If you follow the third sign, turn to page 85.

As you continue along, your spirits rise. In Tenopia's lighter gravity, climbing the mountain trails is easier than it would be on Earth. You finally reach Okur, which is not much more than a collection of sod houses. There are crogocides everywhere!

If you have been to Okur before, turn to page 7. If not, read on. . . .

Before you can do anything, the crogocides grab you and shove you down a flight of stone steps into a dimly lighted cellar. Groping your way along the walls, you find a passageway. You investigate it and quickly perceive that you have entered a maze. You wander through the maze, hoping that somehow you'll find your way to freedom, but you only get more and more lost. You begin to panic, then stop, trying to get hold of yourself. You've got to think of a strategy for getting out of the maze. Two ideas occur to you.

*If you decide to go right at every corner,
turn to page 71.*

*If you decide to alternate your direction,
going right at the first corner, left at the next,
and so on, turn to page 83.*

58

You've decided to head upstream, away from the sea. You walk along the stream for a while. Then, coming upon a road, you follow it west, ready to hide at the first sign of crogocides.

Shortly after crossing the ruins of an ancient wall, you see a far different landscape ahead. You've entered an area of steaming wastes. The air smells of sulfur. The spongy ground gurgles under your feet.

You make your way past boiling geysers. Ahead of you, mists of foul-smelling vapors rise from a crevice spanned by a narrow, sagging wooden bridge. You step back a bit to fill your lungs with air, then cautiously step onto the bridge, praying it won't collapse.

 TO CHECK MAP, SEE PAGE 41.

Turn to page 40.

Within moments you are standing on the bank of the Rapoor River. The water is deep and dark, and you can hardly see below the surface, but the river is only twenty yards wide. You can easily swim that far—the current isn't too swift. You'll just have to hope. . . .

Plunging into the cold black water, you stroke slowly and steadily. In your mind is a picture of a zazor fish homing in on you. Gamely you paddle on.

Now the shore is only a few feet away.

Owww! One got you! You accelerate and scramble out of the water, bleeding. Luckily, the wound isn't serious. The zazor fish only nicked your leg. You rest awhile, get up, and resume your trek, eventually reaching a dirt road.

Turn to page 74.

After a half-day's journey you reach the Land of Nowhere.

If you have been to the Land of Nowhere before, turn to page 123. If not, read on. . . .

Despite its forbidding name, Nowhere is most agreeable. The people seem to have nothing to do but laugh and dance and sing. You join in the frolic, but you can't find anyone who can tell you which way to go.

No one in Nowhere speaks the galactic language. But a friendly bird child teaches you a little of her mountain language. These are the words you learn:

So ("North")   **Nee** ("Yes")
No ("South")   **Yo** ("No")
Wo ("East")   **Co** ("Go")
Et ("West")   **Gom** ("Come")

Suddenly you hear people shouting the one word that is the same in both languages—*crogocides!* They are riding in from the north! That news is enough for you, and you leave Nowhere on the run, headed the other way.

 TO CHECK MAP, SEE PAGE 29.

Turn to page 50.

62

After an easy hike along Lake Shonra you reach the village of Shar. The rounded houses here are decorated with mosaics of different-colored stones. Shar seems pleasant enough, and you decide to stay a few days to rest and think about where to go next. You spend a day working on a fishing boat and become friendly with a bird person named Krug. He doesn't seem very bright, but you feel he is honest.

"Have you ever heard of Zindor, to the east of here?" you ask.

"I don't know if there is any such place," he replies. "But it's dangerous to go east, because you will be in the shadow of the Keona Volcano. It might erupt at any time. I would take the trail north and stay well away from the volcano. Or if you like, I'll take you across the lake; you might find a safer route east from there."

 TO CHECK MAP, SEE NEXT PAGE.

If you head north, turn to page 81.

If you head east, despite Krug's advice, turn to page 84.

If you accept the offer of a ride across the lake, turn to page 88.

You're able to find a trail that winds through the Karra Mountains, and after two days of travel you come upon a beautiful valley. As you follow a path through the meadow you are almost surrounded by long black snakes.

Suddenly they are on you! Dozens of slimy black thrashing things curl and slither around your neck, under your arms, around your legs. As soon as you pry one off, two more coil about you. You yell, but no one is there to hear you. Yet the moment you cry out, the snakes drop back to the grass. They raise their heads several feet in the air and look at you curiously. You breathe a sigh of relief, wipe your brow, and continue on your way, some of the snakes still following like friendly puppies.

In the distance ahead you see a glimpse of water. Checking your map, you can tell that you're looking at the western tip of Lake Shonra. You could take a mountain trail toward the lake, or follow the trails that branch to your left and right.

 TO CHECK MAP, SEE PAGE 41.

If you follow the mountain trail to your left, turn to page 52.

If you follow the mountain trail to your right, turn to page 57.

If you head toward the lake, turn to page 55.

As you travel, the vegetation becomes so dense that you would have to turn back were it not for the narrow trail that winds through the forest.

Rounding a bend, you see an animal ahead—a giant spider several feet high! Three spikes project from its great head. Suddenly it pounces on a small mammal, tosses it with its front legs, then tears it apart.

Shuddering, you pick up a heavy stick from the forest floor. Little use! Ahead of you is a whole army of giant spiders. You turn around, but there are more of them on the route you just traveled! You stumble into the forest, trying to follow a straight line and hoping you'll reach a safe trail.

Then you hear voices ahead. Eagerly, you press on. But your heart sinks—crogocides! Ruefully, you consider that they may be your only hope of escaping the giant spiders.

 TO CHECK MAP, SEE PAGE 41.

If you show yourself to the crogocides and ask for help, turn to page 7.

If you try to cut through the forest and keep clear of the spiders, turn to page 102.

After a day's journey, you arrive in the small fishing village of Sita. It seems strangely quiet. The bird people who live here have a dark blue plumage unlike any blue you've seen before. But only a few are moving about in the narrow streets. Most are sleeping on simple straw mats under low wooden shelters.

If you've been to Sita before, turn to page 113. If not, read on. . . .

Two of the bird people are loading a boat with crates of shellfish, and you wonder where that boat will be going. You try to talk to them, but they go about their business as if you weren't there.

Wandering about the village you find that the few people who aren't sleeping don't seem to talk at all— to you or to each other.

Soon you feel sleepy yourself, so you lie down on an unoccupied straw mat. In an instant you are asleep and dreaming. The dream is the most vivid you've ever had. The people of Sita are all awake and talking. Several of them gather around you, telling stories and patting you on the back with their indigo-tipped wings.

Go on to the next page.

When you awake, nearly everyone is sleeping as before. You're amazed—these bird people seem to live their lives mostly in dreams!

Looking around, you see the two bird people on the boat unloosening the docking lines. Though it's late afternoon, you are well rested from your nap and eager to be on your way.

 TO CHECK MAP, SEE PAGE 29.

If you decide to jump aboard the boat and take your chances, turn to page 86.

If you decide to take the road in the direction of the orange sun, turn to page 33.

If you decide to take the road in the direction away from the orange sun, turn to page 82.

"All right," you say. "As soon as I'm standing in a safe place above ground, I'll give you the secret of my magic."

The crogocide nods. "I'll wake you an hour before dawn and lead you to the surface."

While everyone else is still asleep the guard awakens you. Carrying a torch, he leads you through a long winding tunnel that emerges aboveground some distance from the mine. Once you see that the coast is clear, you have no choice but to hand over your computer and show the guard how to make it work.

The crogocide points toward a path leading into a forest of stubby pines. "This is the mountain trail—it's your best route." Without another word, he disappears back into the tunnel with your computer.

You start walking; there's no other choice.

Turn to page 81.

For what seems like hours you feel your way along through the pitch-black maze, always turning right; then you reach a dead end. The surface in front of you feels like wood. You press against it and it gives way, admitting a flood of light. You walk through the open door—free!

Looking around, you see that you are on the bank of a shallow river, which is running downstream to your left, toward the sea. Your map shows that Lake Shonra lies only a short distance to the northeast. And you remember that Prespar said that Zindor is east of Lake Shonra. Unfortunately the way east is blocked by the Jagged Mountains.

 TO CHECK MAP, SEE PAGE 41.

If you head upstream, turn to page 58.

If you head downstream, turn to page 67.

Once again you have reached the Land of the Miniphants. Determined not to be caught again and hauled off to the mines, you decide to move on quickly. But you can't resist making friends with one of the miniphants. You are patting its trunk when you see what you most feared—crogocides riding toward

you! Suddenly the miniphant kneels down. You climb on its back, and it breaks into a loping run with surprising speed. The crogocides with their clumsy zekees are left far behind.

After an hour's ride through a pretty forest of ferns and hanging moss, the miniphant stops at the beginning of a path and lowers its rump. You slide down its back; it turns, trumpets, and trots back toward its home.

Safe for the moment, you continue on foot along the path.

 TO CHECK MAP, SEE PAGE 29.

Turn to page 61.

You've been walking along the road for several hours when a large cart comes by, driven by a bird man and drawn by two zekees. Unnoticed, you run after it, jump on the back, and crawl under a canvas that's spread over a load of fruit and vegetables! After enjoying a good meal, you fall asleep.

At dawn you awaken. The cart has stopped in a little village. Birds are singing everywhere. The air smells of freshly baked bread. Consulting your map, you decide you must have reached the town of Pira.

You hop off the cart and start walking. Soon you reach a bluff. You look over the edge at big waves crashing on the rocks below. In both directions the coast continues almost in a straight line. Looking left, you stare straight into the early morning sun.

 TO CHECK MAP, SEE PAGE 17.

If you head toward the sun, turn to page 124.

If you head the other way, turn to page 86.

Suddenly you are surrounded by crogocide guards and on your way to the crystal mine.

If you have been enslaved in the crystal mine before, turn to page 34. If not, read on. . . .

The mine entrance looks like the entrance to a cave. The guards march you inside and force you down a great spiral ramp that winds hundreds of feet below ground.

Mining crystal is harder than mining krelium. And noisier! The constant clatter and clinking makes thinking almost impossible. As the dreary, noise-filled days pass, you begin to lose hope.

One day a guard sidles up to you. "I can help you escape," he says in a hushed voice.

You can hardly believe your ears. "Thank you. I would be grateful."

"Don't thank me," the guard answers. "I expect payment. I have heard that you have magic powers—that you can make maps appear from nowhere. Teach me to do that and I will help you."

He wants your computer! "But I can't let you have . . . I mean, I can't teach you that!"

"Then you can stay here forever" is his stern reply.

If you give up your computer in order to escape, turn to page 70.

If you refuse, turn to page 116.

You dive in and just try to keep afloat while the current sweeps you rapidly downstream and out of sight of your pursuers. Then you have to swim hard to make it to shore before the rapids engulf you. You fight to make it to the east bank, but the river deposits you on the other side.

As you climb out of the water, you're thankful for the warmth of the big orange sun. After drying off as much as you can, you head south across the countryside. You decide to give the river a wide berth and put as much ground as you can between yourself and the crogocides.

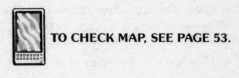 **TO CHECK MAP, SEE PAGE 53.**

Turn to page 92.

Once again you find yourself in the gracious company of the prince of Agron.

"Since I last saw you, I've been thinking about your quest," he says. "I've asked all my subjects and none of them knows how to reach Zindor, but I have learned that there is a monastery in the Dazzling Mountains far to the east, beyond Sita. It is called Chawakelamptha. If you ever get there, ask to see the abbot, and he will show you the way."

You thank the prince and set out again on your journey.

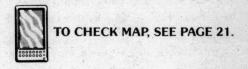 **TO CHECK MAP, SEE PAGE 21.**

If you take the road northeast to Sita,
turn to page 68.

If you take the road southeast to Gerzan,
turn to page 38.

Following the trail marked by crossed logs, you walk along a stream that winds between wooded hills.

At last you reach Chiga, a tiny farming village, where you have your first good meal in a long time. The people are not able to answer your questions, but they take you to a rocky hill near town and point to a great stone marker. You carefully study the words written on it:

Co No

There are three roads leading out of town. One is to the northwest, one to the east, and one to the south.

You feel you must now be very close to Zindor. Before deciding which road to take, you think back about all you've learned during your travels.

 TO CHECK MAP, SEE NEXT PAGE.

If you take the road to the northwest, turn to page 120.

If you take the road to the east, turn to page 75.

If you take the road to the south, turn to page 105.

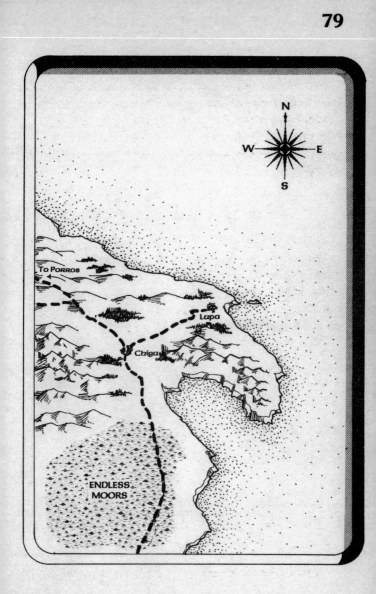

As you travel along, you find yourself climbing higher and higher. The temperature drops. You're going to have to cross a high mountain pass, and a bitter wind is blowing. You wish you had warmer clothes. In fact, you wish you were safe at home. Though you resolve to keep moving, you feel yourself growing steadily weaker. At last you find a rock outcropping that forms a shallow cave. You huddle inside, wondering whether you will ever escape from these mountains, much less this island, much less Tenopia!

You are drifting toward delirium when you hear the banging of gongs. At first the sound is so faint you think you are dreaming, then it grows louder. A band of mountain people is stopping to take shelter in your cave!

The mountain people are as surprised to see you as you are to see them. They wrap you in warm robes and give you broth to drink.

If you have lost your computer, turn to page 121. If not, read on. . . .

When at last the storm subsides, the mountain people guide you to a trail they promise will lead you to a safe place.

Turn to page 95.

82

In time, you reach the village of Noma. The houses of Noma are modest shelters, but the streets and squares and rooftops are dotted with stone statues of bird people and some of the other strange creatures that live on Tenopia Island.

If you have been to Noma before, turn to page 109. If not, read on. . . .

When you ask for food at the central house, the bird people offer to feed you on condition that you make a statue of yourself for the town.

After dining on berry bread and baked fish, you go to work in a studio of the central house. Your hosts are not pleased with your work. They mutter and fret as you chip away at your stone.

Suddenly three crogocides appear at the door! In a moment they're after you. You leap through a window and start running—but your way is blocked by a river. It is flowing very fast and you can hear rapids downstream.

 TO CHECK MAP, SEE PAGE 53.

If you dive in and swim for it, turn to page 76.

If you try to hide in the bushes near the river, turn to page 75.

After hours of fruitless wandering, you take a turn that brings you back to the dark cellar where you started. Exhausted, you sit down and try to decide what to do next.

Turn to page 7.

Determined to move east, you march resolutely over the barren land. The porous gray rock beneath your feet, solidified lava, reminds you that the smoke spewing from the volcano's summit may signal an eruption.

Suddenly the ground rumbles. Tongues of flame are shooting out of the volcano's cone. You start to run, but in a moment the ground is still again and the flames subside.

No wonder the crogocides avoid this area! In a way, you feel safe here—you have only nature to fear. Nevertheless, you dare not get any closer to the volcano. Luckily, up ahead is an old trail, running north-south, that probably skirts the volcano.

 TO CHECK MAP, SEE PAGE 63.

If you head north, turn to page 95.

If you head south, turn to page 91.

You proceed along a winding road until you are confronted by a miniature mountain range of jagged peaks and cliffs. They rise only as high as twenty feet, but it takes forever to get around them. Once in this maze of jagged spires, you can't see very far—you have no idea how far they extend. Your map is no help because there are no other landmarks. You push on blindly with no sense of direction.

Turn to page 94.

86

After an uneventful journey, you reach the town of Rapoor.

If you have been to Rapoor before, turn to page 90. If not, read on. . . .

Set upon a hill above the town and overlooking the sea is a great stone bird tower—an homage to a god that the bird people imagine holds back the stormy sea.

The bird people of Rapoor are unusually shy, but one of them is willing to help you in your search for Zindor.

"If you wish to find your way to the east end of Tenopia Island, avoid the river road," he says.

You thank him for this advice and look at your map for further guidance.

 TO CHECK MAP, SEE PAGE 17.

If you follow the river to the northeast, turn to page 44.

If you follow the road to the southeast, turn to page 74.

If you follow the road northwest to Kacita, turn to page 24.

After a half-day trip, you reach the prettiest village you've seen on Tenopia Island. The houses, which are made of textured stone, are set on a terraced hillside and tinted in blues, greens, and pinks.

If you have been to Medea before, turn to page 129. If not, read on. . . .

You find a place to stay for the night in Medea in the home of a friendly bird woman. She gives you food and shelter in exchange for your weeding her garden and gathering wood for her stove.

"Have you ever heard of Zindor?" you ask.

"Oh, yes," she replies. "It's in the afternoon shadow of the great volcano."

"How do I get there? Can I go east along the lake?"

"The way east is blocked by swamp monsters. You must follow the road south to Tonga," she replies.

The next morning, you bid the bird woman good-bye. As you are setting out, you notice a small sailboat tied up to a dock. You could borrow the boat to sail to the east end of the lake! You're desperate, after all. And the owner can always get the boat later.

 TO CHECK MAP, SEE PAGE 63.

If you take the sailboat and head east down the lake, turn to page 108.

If you follow the road south to Tonga, turn to page 94.

If you follow the road west along the lake, turn to page 55.

You make your way to the base of the stone bird tower of Rapoor, where you pause to check your map. There are three routes out of town: the road northwest to Kacita, the road southeast to Pira, and the river road, which will take you northeast to the Land of the Nekka. Feeling that you've already gained as much information as you're likely to get from the shy natives of Rapoor, you decide to move on.

 TO CHECK MAP, SEE PAGE 17.

If you take the road to Kacita, turn to page 24.

If you take the road to Pira, turn to page 74.

If you follow the river road to the Land of the Nekka, turn to page 44.

You proceed for several hours, forced by the difficult terrain to follow a road that takes you to Sera on the southeast shore of Lake Shonra.

If you have been to Sera before, turn to page 132. If not, read on. . . .

The bird people of Sera tell you of a local shaman who can reveal to you the way to reach Zindor. You visit this kindly old bird man, who lives in a tiny hut. He offers you some mush that tastes like rice and bananas.

"Will you tell me where Zindor is?" you ask.

"Zindor is nestled in the lava fields of the Keona Volcano."

You consult your map. You're practically there!

But the shaman must be reading your mind. "There is no trail from here to Zindor," he says. "Sometimes the true path is not the shortest. If you try to go east, toward Zindor, you will have grave troubles. I advise you to go in the opposite direction. Take a boat west, to Medea, and you will find your way."

 TO CHECK MAP, SEE PAGE 63.

If you head east despite the shaman's advice, turn to page 114.

If you take a boat to Medea, turn to page 88.

You walk for hours until at last you reach open grasslands. Ahead of you is a herd of animals that remind you of elephants, except these are only as big as ponies and their skin is covered with fur. Their trunks have branching tips that serve as fingers and thumb.

If you have been to the Land of the Miniphants before, turn to page 73. If not, read on. . . .

Go on to the next page.

You can tell that these miniphants are both dexterous and intelligent, for they have obviously built the log shelters that dot the landscape. You watch with amazement as several miniphants stack logs, while others rip branches off fallen trees. One of the animals comes up and nuzzles you with her trunk.

But suddenly the miniphants start running. What could have frightened them? Looking around, you see crogocides mounted on their zekees, riding toward you! In a moment a net descends over your head. You know that means only one thing—slavery.

To your surprise, they let you choose between serving in the krelium mine or in the crystal mine that lies to the east.

You're horrified at the thought of going back to the krelium mine and beginning your quest all over again. Still, there's a good chance of escape from there if the secret tunnel hasn't been sealed.

If you choose the krelium mine, turn to page 7.

If you choose the crystal mine, turn to page 75.

In time, you reach the area called Tonga.

If you have been to Tonga before, turn to page 125. If not, read on. . . .

There's not even a village here—only meadows and simple farms, nestled against the rain forest that lies to the east. The bird people who live on the farms are afraid to enter the forest, which they tell you is inhabited by apelike creatures that sometimes come out and snatch children to eat.

The story about the ape creatures sounds like a myth to you. You're inclined to ignore it. On the other hand . . .

 TO CHECK MAP, SEE PAGE 63.

If you head east through the rain forest, turn to page 97.

If you go south in hopes of finding a safer route along the coast, turn to page 102.

If you head north, turn to page 88.

Walking through high grazing lands, you meet shepherds herding flocks of nambats—animals whose fur is shorn and made into warm clothes and blankets. The shepherds are isolated mountain folk who speak their own strange tongue.

They take you in and give you food and drink. They understand you want directions, but seem puzzled about what you're looking for. At last, one of the shepherds smiles as if he understands. He leads you to a place where the trail forks left and right.

Pointing to your left he says, "Co Chawakelamptha." Pointing to your right he says, "Yo Co Porros."

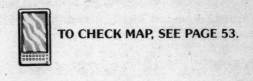 **TO CHECK MAP, SEE PAGE 53.**

If you take the trail to the left, turn to page 99.

If you take the trail to the right, turn to page 120.

You sleep well that night at the Chawakelamptha monastery and set out the next day. The trail winds downhill most of the way, and you reach the cave of the four monks shortly before dark. The monks—Ao, Ra, Tig, and Chi—greet you warmly and offer you dinner and a bed for the night.

When you ask the way to Zindor, they answer you as follows:

Ao says, "Take the trail marked by three rock pillars."

Ra says, "Ao is lying. Take the trail marked by a solitary pine tree."

Tig says, "Ao and Ra are both lying. Take the trail marked by two logs, fastened by vines to make a cross."

Chi says, "Tig is lying. It is Ao who told the truth."

Ra adds, "Alas, I remember now—it *is* the trail marked by the three rock pillars."

If you decide to take the trail marked by the three rock pillars, turn to page 101.

If you decide to take the trail marked by a solitary pine, turn to page 120.

If you decide to take the trail marked by two logs fastened to make a cross, turn to page 78.

With a feeling close to fear, you trudge into the rain forest. As you wade through tall ferns you keep looking up into the shaggy-bark trees.

Suddenly you see them—huge primates with long orange-brown hair. At least three of them are peering at you from behind trees. They have gentle faces. They don't look like flesh-eaters to you. As you proceed, more ape people come out of the woods. They move closer. With your heart in your mouth, you press forward, but the apes block your way. You understand. They will not hurt you, but neither will they let you pass through their homeland.

Retreating, you quickly project your map before deciding which way to go.

 TO CHECK MAP, SEE PAGE 63.

If you head north, turn to page 91.

If you head south, turn to page 102.

After a trek through the Dazzling Mountains, whose ice-coated spires flash and sparkle with all the colors of the rainbow, you come at last upon three buildings connected by passageways so as to form a perfect triangle.

If you have been to Chawakelamptha before, turn to page 104. If not, read on. . . .

You knock loudly on the door. An old bird man wearing a long gray robe appears. He beckons you to enter. Others dressed the same way join him. They feed you fruit bread and nectar and let you bathe in a great clay tub filled with water heated on a huge wood stove. You learn that your hosts are monks who have retreated from the worldly ways of life in the valleys below.

Frias, the abbot, listens attentively while you describe your wanderings in search of Zindor.

"This is Chawakelamptha," he says. "We live here because we believe it to be the most beautiful place in the universe—the gateway to heaven."

Turn to page 103.

Kin Rugg smiles broadly as the balloon drifts along.

"What about the great storms that sink ships—can we avoid them?" you ask.

"The storms occur close to the surface. We shall fly above them," Kin Rugg replies. But then he adds, "It's true we'll need a bit of luck."

Soon the island is just a hazy speck on the horizon. You're not home yet, but you don't have any doubt you're going to make it. You've shown you have what it takes, and you're ready for whatever adventures await you on the planet Tenopia.

The End

In time, you reach the village of Verde. The people here cast furtive glances at you, then slink away when you move toward them. Even if anyone would talk to you, you'd hesitate to ask for help. You feel you can't trust anyone in this village.

But then an old woman walks right up to you. She seems to have come from another planet, as you did. Her face has a triangular shape that you can't associate with other hominids you've seen on Tenopia Island. "You look as if you need help," she says.

When you tell her your story she nods wisely. "Between here and Zindor lie the Dazzling Mountains," she says. "You can go around them, to the east or to the west."

"Which is best?" you demand.

In a singsong voice, she replies, "East is least and west is best if reason must rhyme."

 TO CHECK MAP, SEE PAGE 53.

If you go west, turn to page 82.

If you go east, turn to page 120.

If you find your way to Chawakelamptha, turn to page 99.

As you travel on in search of a route to Zindor, you have to follow winding animal trails through chest-high vegetation. The lush landscape is punctuated by tall, skinny trees with enormous umbrellalike leaves. Birds with striking gold and silver plumage hover overhead, occasionally diving into the brush to capture small prey.

When at last you reach a high ridge you find yourself looking down on a beautiful harbor. A sailing vessel is lying at anchor not far offshore. At the edge of the water is an encampment. And only a few dozen yards away from you is a group of hominids. They are not crogocides, but they are armed with spears and slings. You're not sure what military group this is, but you know that once you enter their preserve, your fate will be in their hands.

If you show yourself, turn to page 36.

If you retreat the way where you are least likely to be spotted, turn to page 94.

After agreeing with Frias about the beauty of Cha-wakelamptha, you ask his advice on how to proceed.

"There are many trails down the mountain, and they lead many ways," he replies. "Maps are of little help here, so listen carefully. When you leave tomorrow, take the trail that starts from the great rock spire to the north of here. By dusk you will reach a cave shared by four monks, who will give you food and shelter.

"Farther down, the trail divides into three separate trails. To reach Zindor you must pass through Chiga. Each monk knows the way. *But only one will tell the truth.* The other three will always lie, because they will not want you to travel over sacred ground. It's up to you to figure out which monk is telling the truth."

Thanking Frias for his help, you turn in for the night.

 TO CHECK MAP, SEE PAGE 53.

Turn to page 96.

Once again you have reached the monastery of Chawakelamptha.

The abbot, Frias, greets you with a smile. "Perhaps you did not believe the right monk," he says. "Well, next time remember that only one of them ever tells the truth, so you can be sure that if any two monks agree about anything, then those two must be lying."

 TO CHECK MAP, SEE PAGE 53.

Turn to page 96.

After a two-day journey through the moors that dominate the east end of the island, you arrive at Riva.

If you have been to Riva before, turn to page 117. If not, read on. . . .

In talking to the bird people who live in Riva, you learn that, years ago, the islanders here built ships that they hoped could safely cross the great ocean. But of all the ships that set forth, none was ever heard from again.

Unfortunately, the bird people you talk to aren't willing to help you in your quest. Suspecting that they've been intimidated by the crogocides, you decide not to move on until you have clear information about where to go next. You get a job on a fishing boat, letting out and hauling in nets. After work, you hang around the docks, hoping to pick up information.

Go on to the next page.

One day you notice a mural painted on the wall of a dockside tavern. While you are looking at the mural, a bird man runs in yelling, "The crogocides are coming!"

You have only a minute to consult your map, and this is no time to make a mistake!

 TO CHECK MAP, SEE PAGE 47.

If you head east, turn to page 46.

If you head west, turn to page 118.

If you head south, turn to page 114.

You unhitch the boat from the dock, raise the sail, and head toward the east end of the lake. But you're soon forced off course by strong winds. The boat has a strange rig, and you can't seem to manage it. Soon you're being blown out toward the center of the lake and far to the west.

The waves grow higher. Spray comes over the side. You forget about trying to get anywhere—you just want to make it safely to shore. To make matters worse, a dense fog is sweeping across the lake. "Why did I do this?" you shout.

The boat is hard to sail, but it's solid and sound, and when the wind subsides, you are still afloat. You drift through the night and finally reach a deserted shore just before dawn. As soon as light comes, you start walking.

 TO CHECK MAP, SEE PAGE 63.

Turn to page 85.

The bird people of Noma welcome you back with open wings.

Hurrick, a stonecutter, is friendly toward you. You tell him your story and ask for his help.

"I don't know where Zindor lies," says Hurrick, "but I'll be glad to show you how to find a trail to wherever else you'd like to go."

 TO CHECK MAP, SEE PAGE 53.

If you ask Hurrick to show you the way . . .

to Mount Calm, turn to page 52;

to Verde, turn to page 101;

to Porros, turn to page 120;

to Chawakelamptha, turn to page 99;

to a path that leads across the Dazzling Mountains, turn to page 81.

Over the wall you jump. As your feet hit the ground, you sense that you've made the wrong move. Peering through the brush is another human, but he scampers into the woods like a frightened animal.

You pass some old bird people sitting in a circle, chewing on roots. Nearby, a giant sloth is standing on its hind legs, gnawing at the bark of a tree. Continuing on, you see other creatures. They all seem to be living in a world of their own—as if they have been there a very long time.

You walk on through land covered with beautiful mosses and ferns but barren of trees. Soon afterward you reach the top of a 300-foot-high cliff. From it you gaze down at the huge waves breaking against the rocks below. Walking along first in one direction, then in the other, you find that the wall from which you jumped seals off a narrow peninsula entirely bound by high cliffs. Slowly it dawns on you: this must be Cape Mori. Only now do you remember Prespar's warning. You've jumped into a trap—a prison from which you may never escape.

Go on to the next page.

112

The weather is mild, and you build a lean-to that gives you a comfortable shelter for sleeping. Delicious breadfruit, berries, and nuts grow everywhere, so you have no fear of starving to death. But neither do you have any hope of being rescued. And as the days go by, you grow increasingly depressed.

One day, as you are walking through a meadow, you trip on a rock and fall on your face, almost banging your head on another rock. The whole meadow is strewn with rocks, many of them small enough to carry. You realize you can build a staircase to the top of the wall!

You pick up a rock and carry it to the wall. Then you go back and get another. You lay them side by side. You go back and get another rock, then another, and another, and another. You work all the rest of that day and most of the next and the next and the next.

At last your staircase is built. Joyfully you climb to the top and descend the buttress on the other side. You are free of your prison, but you still have a long way to go to escape from Tenopia Island. There's nothing to do now but start walking.

Turn to page 102.

Sita looks just the way you remember it, except there is no boat being readied to leave port. Hoping to learn something by dreaming, you pick an unoccupied straw mat and lie down. Once again sleep comes, quickly bringing a dream about the friendly, blue bird people. In your dream, the bird people interrupt their lively chatter to listen attentively to your questions. But before you can hear any answers, a new dream is upon you—a vision of a great volcano, smoke rising from its snow-capped cone. As if you were flying near it, you look down and see the porous black lava fields at the base of the mountain. Nestled in a valley spared by the lava flow is a tiny village. A large balloon rises from the village and drifts slowly toward the distant sea. As quickly as it began, this dream is replaced by another: you are back in the village of Sita. The bird people are standing nearby, chattering excitedly. One of them screams. You look around. Dozens of crogocides, holding nets and spears, are charging toward you. Suddenly you wake up in a cold sweat! The scene around you is as quiet and peaceful as ever. But you have no doubt you should get out of town in a hurry. You quickly rise from your mat and head east at a brisk pace.

Turn to page 82.

114

For hours you travel through swampy, squishy land spotted with dead trees and sinkholes, from which smoke and steam pour forth. You dazedly make your way over the difficult terrain, choking on the fumes. Suddenly you slip, twisting your ankle, and fall into a pit. You lie for a moment at the bottom of the steaming pit, rubbing your throbbing ankle, then frantically search the sides of the pit for a handhold. Nothing. You raise your eyes—and see a triangular-headed creature staring at you from the lip of the pit. You shrink back, but then you remember something you heard on your travels. This must be a volca! These intelligent and friendly creatures live solely on ammonia. Their habitat is limited to a few places where no other creature would survive.

Another volca quickly joins the first. Swinging their powerful tails down into the pit, they swiftly pull you up to the surface. They carry you to the edge of their habitat, where grass and trees begin to grow, and you rest there while your ankle is mending.

In a few days, your ankle feels fine, and thanks to the volcas, you're able to move on. The ammonia fumes are too strong for you to go north, and the route south is blocked by cliffs and canyons.

 TO CHECK MAP, SEE PAGE 47.

If you head east, turn to page 46.

If you head west, turn to page 91.

Deciding that you must hold on to your computer at all costs, you decline the guard's offer and resign yourself to an indefinite sentence at hard labor. Someday, you vow, you'll find a chance to escape.

In the days ahead, security becomes tighter than ever. Guards watch you day and night. When you have a chance to talk to some of the other prisoners, ones who have been there a long time, they all say the same thing: there is no hope.

You won't give up hope—that's all you have left. Yet, as the days pass, you find yourself becoming increasingly depressed. Then one day you are awakened much earlier than usual and brought before one of the crogocide overseers. "We have more workers here than we need and not enough in the krelium mine," he tells you. "Tomorrow you will be transferred, and it is in the krelium mine, not here, where you will spend the rest of your life."

This is hardly good news; yet it's enough to rekindle your spirits. And you still have your computer.

Turn to page 7.

Once again you've arrived at Riva, on the east coast of Tenopia Island. This time you're determined to take the right trail.

You're sure by now that Zindor lies practically in the shadow of the great Keona Volcano.

You study your map carefully before making your decision.

 TO CHECK MAP, SEE PAGE 47.

If you head east, turn to page 46.

If you head west, turn to page 118.

If you head south, turn to page 114.

As you head west, you soon find yourself climbing along a narrow ridge, which falls off steeply on either side into impassable lava fields. You realize you must be nearing the base of the Keona Volcano. Stopping on the narrow ridge you raise your eyes skyward. A heavy plume of smoke is rising from the volcano's summit, and you don't relish the thought of approaching more closely.

You step forward slowly—and almost stumble over a crogocide lying in the grass. He seems to have fallen asleep while guarding the trail. What is there to guard? you wonder. Your heart leaps with anticipation. You tiptoe past the guard and continue on. Ahead, the ridge curves. Walking quickly you reach the curve and look down onto a beautiful valley nearly surrounded by mounds of solidified lava. In the center of the valley is a cluster of neatly crafted houses.

As you walk into the tiny settlement, a hominid of the same species as Prespar comes forward to meet you. "My name is Kin Rugg. Welcome to Zindor," he says.

Go on to the next page.

From your pocket you pull a crumpled and barely legible letter. "Prespar sent me to ride in his place on the balloon trip to Kabran," you explain.

Kin Rugg reads the letter and nods. "I never break a promise. Besides, I am tired of hiding from the crogocides. You may stay at my home tonight. Tomorrow at dawn we shall leave Tenopia Island forever."

Turn to page 126.

120

After a considerable hike, you reach Porros. As you are about to enter the village, guards emerge from a shelter by the side of the road.

Your heart sinks as several crogocides gallop up on their shaggy zekees.

Turn to page 7.

As you wait out the storm, huddled with the mountain people for warmth, one of them pulls a familiar-looking object from his sack. You let out a cry of surprise. It's your computer!

"Is yours?" he asks, handing it to you.

"Yes, yes! Thank you. Where did you find it?"

The mountain person laughs. "Crogocide open this. Poof! Ow! Ow! Ow!" As he speaks, the mountain person imitates a crogocide trying to open something, jumping back as if from an explosion, and throwing the thing down. The guard who took your computer must have tried to open it and gotten an electric shock!

You amuse the mountain people by showing them how you can project a map of the region. Fortunately they know the land so well, they have no interest in keeping the computer for themselves.

The storm subsides, and the mountain people guide you to a trail they promise will lead to a safe place.

Turn to page 95.

You see the humble sod houses and the dragon statue of Leata. When you enter the village, the chattering bird people surround you, happy to see you again. But their directions to Zindor are still of no use to you. Once again, you consult your map.

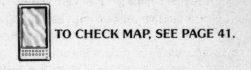 **TO CHECK MAP, SEE PAGE 41.**

If you take the road to Okur,
turn to page 57.

If you take the road around Mount Karra,
turn to page 55.

Once again you hear music and laughter as you enter the Land of Nowhere. Your spirits rise. Now that you know some of their language, you should be able to get directions.

Then you hear a shout: "Crogocides! *So!*"

So means "north," you remember, and you quickly turn and run the other way.

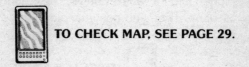 **TO CHECK MAP, SEE PAGE 29.**

Turn to page 50.

You walk east along the coast road, crossing the ruins of an ancient wall. After a few hours, you come upon the mouth of a narrow river that marks the beginning of a vast jungle north of the road.

You pause to decide whether or not it's safe to swim across. Then you hear a shout from behind you. A crogocide! There's no other choice: you plunge into the warm, muddy water and swim to the far bank. Then you continue along the coast road.

 TO CHECK MAP, SEE PAGE 41.

Turn to page 102.

Back in Tonga, you visit one of the farmhouses to ask advice on your next move.

The bird people tell you that the road west leads to Issus. You check your map for other clues. The road north leads to Medea, on Lake Shonra; the road south leads to a harbor, and the road east leads to the rain forest.

 TO CHECK MAP, SEE PAGE 63.

If you take the road . . .

to Medea, turn to page 88;

to Issus, turn to page 55;

to the rain forest, turn to page 97;

to the harbor, turn to page 102.

As the huge orange sun rises above the eastern hills, Kin Rugg casts off the lines on the great balloon. It rises rapidly—almost as high as the Keona Volcano—while strong upper winds carry you safely north of Riva, over the moors and the rocky coast, and out over the great ocean.

Turn to page 100.

128

You remember how easy it is to climb to the top of the wall. Whether or not you want to get to the other side is a different story. Before deciding what to do next, you look at your map and see that three roads lead away from the wall. The road north goes to Riva, the road west leads to the Land of Volcas, and the southwestern road leads toward the coast.

 TO CHECK MAP, SEE PAGE 47.

If you take the road toward Riva, turn to page 75.

If you head toward the Land of Volcas, turn to page 114.

If you go southwest, toward the coast, turn to page 102.

If you climb over the wall, turn to page 111.

Once again you have reached the beautiful village of Medea.

If the last time you were here, you took a sailboat without asking for it, the bird people turn you over to the crogocides. In that case, turn to page 7. If not, read on. . . .

The friendly bird woman greets you with open wings. This time she takes you to an ancient creature named Mi.

Go on to the next page.

Mi sits cross-legged on a mat. She has lost most of her feathers, and her skin has shrunk so much that in places it has split, revealing patches of bloodless blue flesh. For a long time she stares at you until you wonder whether she is still conscious, or even alive. But finally she speaks.

"Yes, I know where Zindor is—just east of the Keona Volcano, so close that the crogocides dare not visit it. But between here and there is a swamp you can never cross. To reach Zindor you must find Chawakelamptha. It lies to the north, in the Dazzling Mountains."

Turn to page 133.

You decide not to stay long in Sera. Instead, you plan to move on to one of the nearby villages along the shore of Lake Shonra in search of new information about the route to Zindor.

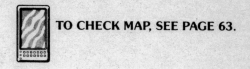

TO CHECK MAP, SEE PAGE 63.

If you take a boat west to Medea,
turn to page 88.

If you hike around the lake to Shar,
turn to page 62.

Mi falls silent; you know you have learned all you can from her. The next morning you set out again to reach the Dazzling Mountains. Since you'll have to go around the western end of Lake Shonra, you follow the road west. After walking several hours you come to a fork in the road.

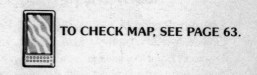 **TO CHECK MAP, SEE PAGE 63.**

If you take the road to the left, turn to page 85.

If you continue straight ahead, turn to page 55.

ABOUT THE AUTHOR

EDWARD PACKARD is a graduate of Princeton University and Columbia Law School. He is the creator of Bantam's Escape™ and Choose Your Own Adventure® series and the author of many books for children.

ABOUT THE ILLUSTRATOR

DAVID PERRY studied art in New York and Rome. He has written and illustrated a book for children, *The Grox and Eugene*, in addition to illustrating books and periodicals.

CHOOSE YOUR OWN ADVENTURE

Prices and availability subject to change without notice.